THE DAYS AFTER

A Tschaaa Infestation Novella

MARSHALL MILLER

Blue Forge Press
Port Orchard ❀ Washington

The Days After
May 2025
by Marshall Miller

First Print Edition May 2025

ISBN 979-889439-044-4

For information about subsidiary rights, contact: blueforgegroup@gmail.com

Blue Forge Press is the print division of the volunteer-run, federal 501(c)(3) nonprofit company, Blue Legacy, founded in 1989. We strive to empower storytellers across all walks of life with our four divisions: Blue Forge Press, Blue Forge Films, Blue Forge Gaming, and Blue Forge Sound. Find out more at www. BlueForgeGroup.org

Blue Forge Press
7419 Ebbert Drive Southeast
Port Orchard, Washington 98367
blueforgepress@gmail.com
360-550-2071 ph.txt

The Tschaaa Infestation Series

Novels & Novellas
Survivors
The Days After
The Gathering Storm
The Tsunami
Typhoon of Steel

Short Story Collections
Free Range Protocol
Beyond the Great Compromise

Games
The Days After: A Build-a-Board Game
The Days After: Indigo Expansion

THE DAYS AFTER

A *Tschaaa Infestation* Novella

MARSHALL MILLER

THE MENU

The darkness was so complete, it felt suffocating. No moonlight filtered in, no glow of city lights—only shadows pressing in on every side.

"Breaking news! Meteorites have struck all over the world. Here in the United States: Atlanta, New York, and Seattle are in flames. Film at eleven."

Jeanie Parker's memory echoed with the broadcaster's last words as she stumbled forward, the weight of panic pressing against her chest. She stumbled through the pitch-black room, bumping into chairs and tables. Her breath came fast and uneven, her flashlight trembling in one hand, a long-bladed knife gripped in the other.

"Come on, you damn flashlight. Work!" she hissed, slapping

the side of the plastic casing.

The beam finally flickered to life, casting shaky light over a room in disarray—overturned chairs, a table, several storage bins. Jeanie moved slowly, eyes darting, every creak and thump drawing her knife up.

A chair toppled somewhere behind her.

"Fuck!" someone cursed from the dark.

Jeanie froze. "Who's there? I have a big knife and know how to use it!"

"Jeanie?! Is that you?"

Jeanie's heart caught in her throat. "Indigo?! Wh-what! How did you get here?!"

Indigo Dax emerged from

the gloom, her features sharpening in the flashlight's beam. A plastic garbage bag crinkled in her grip, and the breath Jeanie hadn't realized she was holding finally rushed out. They met in a one-armed embrace, relief and disbelief crackling between them. They laughed—too hard, maybe—to push back the fear.

"Man, am I glad to see you," Indigo said, pulling a chair into the center of the room. "I was beginning to think I was the last person alive since I left the Aquarium."

Jeanie nodded, eyes scanning the room even as she listened. "You stayed at work? It was my day off. I felt pretty lucky after I heard that—"

"—that a giant rock hit the Smith Tower? Yeah. That's when I hid out in the Aquarium basement.”

“How long did you hide?”

“Two days, I think? Then I bugged out. I needed to eat.”

Indigo shook the bag in her hand, plastic rustling. She plopped down on the chair and opened it.

Jeanie’s eyes tracked the bag. “You’ve got food?”

“From a Stop ’n’ *Rob*. It was busted wide open, but most of the food was still there.” Indigo hesitated. “There was blood all over the floor. No sign of the owners.”

Jeanie pulled up a chair, her stomach growling at the sight.

Indigo noticed. “Hey girl, I’m sorry. You need something to eat, yeah?”

“I had my last soda this

morning." Jeanie set down the knife and flashlight on the box beside them.

Smiling, Indigo dug through the bag and pulled out a Twinkie. She handed it over. Jeanie took it and tore into the wrapper with a hunger that bordered on desperation.

"You know Twinkies last forever," Indigo said, cracking open a soda. "Where'd you get that knife?" she asked, nodding toward Jeanie's blade.

"It's from my Dad's collection. I grabbed it when I had to leave the house."

"What happened?"

Jeanie swallowed and looked down. "Rock fragments hit my neighborhood and set off all these fires everywhere but the firemen were all busy dealing with the damage from the larger strikes. I took off down the street. My parents weren't home. I was supposed to meet them."

"Did you?"

Jeanie shook her head. "No... they never showed." She shivered. "I grabbed a portable radio and managed to get an AM station. There's no cell reception, no internet."

Indigo frowned. "What'd ya hear on the radio? I haven't heard anything."

Jeanie's face turned grim. "You don't know about the ATVs from Hell? Or the aliens?"

"Aliens? Uh... I heard screams when I tried to go upstairs,

so I went back down to the Aquarium basement. I thought it was riot-
ers."

"You mean you don't know?
Indigo. There are... *things*... after
us."

Indigo blinked. "What the
hell? When I finally came out of hiding, there was smoke in the air from
all the fires but nothing else. I just
started looking for food."

Jeanie bit her lip. "There are
real, live, outer space aliens out
there hunting us. The last report I
heard said they shot rocks at us
from space. Then followed that
with these flying saucer things."

"Damn! What do they look
like?"

"I only saw one of their vehicles. It's a six-wheeled mechanical

monster. All these round heads, and each one is a spotlight. I saw it chase a woman into an alley."

"Oh my god! What did you do?"

"I ran like hell! That's when I dropped the radio. Two days ago."

They sat in silence, chewing slowly.

"You didn't hear... anything?" Jeanie asked.

"Not really. I've been sleeping in cars and empty buildings. That's why I came into this old office. I haven't seen anyone. Do you know anything more?"

Jeanie nodded. "You're not going to believe this but... remember Fred the Octopus?"

"Of course. At the Aquarium.

He kept pulling a Houdini and sneaking out of his tank. Fred liked to snack on the other fish until we padlocked the cover on his tank."

Jeanie's face was intense, her eyes unblinking. "The aliens? The guy on AM radio said they look like Fred."

"That's nuts. Cephalopods from space? For real?"

"For real."

"Why are they here? Why Earth?"

"The guy said... he said... they came to *eat* us."

Indigo reeled. "That can't be a thing. How can they chase us on land?! Fred couldn't do that!"

"Those vehicles can. And the radio guy? He called the aliens

Squids. He saw them do this crab-walk type thing on land. And that's not all. He said... he said the Squids prefer to eat humans with... darker skin."

"Fuck that! Klu Klux Klan from space? Aryan Brotherhood from Uranus? No way. Somebody's smokin' some bad weed."

"Indigo, listen. This is for real. You saw blood, right? And no bodies? Where did everybody go?"

They locked eyes. Indigo straightened, standing tall. "Well, this Black woman will not go down without a fight."

Jeanie retrieved her knife and flashlight, standing shoulder to shoulder with Indigo, muscles tense. "I've got your back, my bestie."

A slippery, wet sound echoed through the darkness.

"What was that?" Indigo asked, inching closer.

"Who's there?! I have a knife—"

A deafening crack split the silence as the shadows burst open. Glossy, black-green tentacles erupted from the darkness, glistening with a slick, briny film. They whipped through the air with sickening speed and weight, slamming into the girls with the wet, rubbery smack of living muscle.

Jeanie barely had time to scream before she was on the ground, wind knocked from her chest, the cold reek of alien flesh filling her nostrils. Her flashlight and knife were sent skittering across the floor and darkness swallowed the room.

Indigo screamed as Jeanie's shrieks echoed.

"Indigo?!" Jeanie's voice cracked with urgency.

Silence fell for a moment, shattered only by Jeanie's escalating sobs as terror gave way to grief.

"Why didn't it take me? Why... why not me?!"

LUCKY SEVEN

Jeanie Parker worked her way through the thick Northwest Washington forest. The red-headed twenty-something tried to be as stealthy as possible as she moved among the bushes and trees. Jeanie was still in a daze as she came to grips with losing her best friend, Indigo Dax. One moment, they were together, stuffing Twinkies in their mouths. Then, the alien Squids found their office building hiding place.

Tentacles slithered out of the darkness and grabbed the two young women. Next, Jeanie was released and rejected, while Indigo was taken. All because Indigo was Black—at least, that was what the radio broadcast reported.

The cephalopod Tschaaa seemed to like the taste of dark-skinned humans over all other prey. How could that even be a thing?! Didn't all humans taste the same?!

Jeanie's eyes filled with tears as she considered the possible reality that Indigo had been some hideous alien's meal.

"No, damn it!" the young woman cried out. "She's not dead. I'll find her and save her!"

"Keep yelling like that, and the Squids will find you, young lady." The voice from out of the brush was not loud but firm and commanding. It was also definitively male.

Jeanie jumped back in surprise and held up her long-bladed knife. "Stay back! I have a knife and know how to use it."

"Hey, lady. Master Gunnery Sergeant Torbin Bender here. I'm a good guy."

"I don't know that! The radio reported renegade humans helping the Squids. Stay back!"

A very muscular male in a camouflage uniform stepped from concealment. Jeanie saw he held an assault rifle but still held her ground. She tried to stand as tall as she could, although there was no way she could look as large as the Gunnery Sergeant.

Torbin Bender smiled as he slung his weapon, then held his hands out, palms up, as he slowly moved toward the redhead. "See, the rifle is put away. How about we make nice—"

"Stay back," yelled Jeanie as she lunged towards Torbin, knife point first.

Torbin's eyes turned steely gray as he looked directly into Jeanie's eyes. "Okay, I have no time to screw around—"

The next thing Jeanie realized, she was flat on her back, with her knife hand wrist aching and a combat boot on her throat. Through blurred vision, she saw the Marine was examining her knife.

"Nice steel. It's a shame you really do not know how to use its potential." Torbin looked down at Jeannie as she struggled to move his foot off her neck. "If I let you up and give you back your blade, will you make nice? I said we are on the same side." He paused. "I'll take that gurgle sound as a yes." Torbin removed his combat boot from Jeannie's neck, and she sat up, coughing a bit and rubbing her throat. "Want some water, young lady?"

Jeannie nodded affirmatively, and Torbin tossed her a plastic water bottle. The redhead took a long drink, then looked the Marine in his eyes. "Can I have my knife now?"

"You going to play nice?"

"Yes, sir."

Torbin threw the knife, so it stuck in the ground between Jeanie's outstretched legs.

Jeanie looked at the knife, then back at Torbin. "I guess I could be dead right now if you were with the Squids."

"Yep. Or hog-tied so you could be eaten later."

Jeanie slowly stood up, then bent over and recovered her knife. She stuck the blade back under the belt, then wiped her hand and offered it to the Marine. "Jeannie Parker, Gunny. Sorry about the… misunderstanding."

Torbin took the offered hand in a friendly shake as he grinned. "So someone taught you about Marine Corp rank, I see."

"My Uncle Ray. My Dad called him the Jarhead's Posterboy."

Torbin chuckled as he sized up the woman in front of him. "Well, you have guts and spirit.

With a bit of hardcore training, you might be able to get some payback on the Squids. I get the impression You have some personal experience with them."

Jeannie blinked back some tears as she replied, "They found Indigo and me hiding in an office building. I'd already seen their vehicles grabbing people. I heard the broadcasts about what they... ate." Jeanie choked back a sob. "They took her because she was Black. They kicked me loose. I... I feel that she is still alive."

"Could be, Jeannie. We have some intel that the Squids and renegade humans are collecting breeding stock."

"Then I really have to get moving and find her—"

"Whoa there. I'm out here with some others collecting survivors. We're headed to an Air Force Base in Montana. Wanna come and learn how to kick Squid's ass? Then you can actually do some damage when you find your friend."

"Yeah. Sure. It's better than moping around. Have you kicked some ass yet?"

"Yeah. I got some payback in Yuma, Arizona. Lost some good troops there but got some payback. First steps can be tiny."

Jeannie paused, then spoke. "So, where do I sign up, Gunny?"

"Follow me, young lady. I'll find you a recruiter."

Jeannie tried to keep up with the Gunny and soon discovered the man was entirely at home, moving through the thick forest. An hour later, they slid into a small clearing around an abandoned cabin of some sort. A Ghillie-suited figure slid from the shadows to greet them. "New meat, Gunny?" a muffled feminine voice inquired.

"Yep, Corporal Hansen. She's been to see the elephant and now wants some payback."

"Huh. The head shed will want to debrief her."

"That's for sure." Torbin motioned to Jeannie. "Into the cabin. We'll get you some hot chow."

Jeannie soon wolfed down

the contents of a heated MRE stew pouch. Food never tasted so good. A now non-Ghillie-wearing Corporal Hansen sat cross-legged beside her with a steaming cup of coffee.

"Family military?" asked Barbara Hansen.

"Some. How about you?"

Barbara laughed. "Nah. College professor type. They were pissed when I signed up with the Corps." The still partially camouflaged face went dark. "They were at Evergreen State College, south of Seattle. I heard it took a direct hit from a piece of space rock."

Jeannie swallowed a hunk of stew. "I was near Seattle proper. Smith Tower took a direct hit, too. I hid, but the Squids still found me."

"Gunny said you lost a friend."

Jeannie paused and blinked back tears. "Yeah. My best friend, Indigo. I feel she is still alive."

The dirty blonde-haired Barbara fixed her with a hard stare. "If you want payback, just remember one thing. Your payback ain't worth someone's life."

Jeannie returned the gaze and saw the steel in the young woman's eyes. "Yeah, Corporal. Got it."

A muscular figure stood over her as she finished her MRE. "Here," said Torbin. "Spare sleeping bag. You keep it with you as your first issued piece of equipment. Lose it, you sleep cold."

"Yes, Gunny." Jeannie took it and saw the brownish-red stains on it. She said nothing as she ignored the blood.

"Get some sleep. We move at first light. With you, we are now seven in number. Seven is supposedly a lucky number." Torbin turned away. "Don't screw up the concept."

Jeannie found a small stack of pine boughs for a mattress and soon fell asleep. Indigo came to her in her dreams. Her best friend reached out to her—

A rough hand shook her awake.

"No crying in your sleep, Troop," said Torbin. "Bad for morale and worse for noise security. Same with loud snoring."

"Yes, Gunny."

She watched as the Marine went to his sleeping bag. "He'll help me find you, Bestie," she mumbled. "He'll make me tough." Jeannie closed her eyes and fell into a dreamless sleep.

From the shadows, Torbin watched.

"Damn, I feel old," he said as he rolled over into his sleeping bag.

Unknown miles away, an ankle-chained figure stirred in her sleep in a darkened room.

Suddenly, Indigo jerked

awake from her fitful slumber on a lumpy mattress and sat up, scream-ing.

"Jeanie!"

DRILL, FIGHT, REPEAT

Jeanie Parker forced her tired legs to move her body and the seventy-pound pack up the road to the back gate of Malmstrom Armed Forces Base. Part of Jeanie's military training required that she knew Malmstrom had been a U.S. Air Force Base, even at one time having a nuclear-armed ICBM field. Now, it was the central command and control base of the Unoccupied States of America.

Gunny Sergeant Torbin Bender had begun Jeanie's training, and then Corporal, now Staff Sergeant Barbara Hansen, had continued it. Jeannie humped a heavy pack along with twenty-nine other new members of the Unoccupied States of America Combined Military. Some had prior military experience, but most did not. Their ages varied from eighteen to thirty years plus some years. Torbin and the powers-that-be had decided anyone wanting to fight the Squids needed updated training. Part of this training was to disburse anyone from simply wanting payback.

Jeanie looked forward to a hot shower once this exercise terminated. She knew she must smell like a pig.

"Alright, close it up!" bellowed Sergeant Hansen. "Time for some military decorum as we enter the base. We will *not* look like a gaggle of geese."

Many of Jeanie's trainee cohorts grumbled under their breaths and hoped Hansen did not hear them. The Training Instructor hated whiners and complainers. After five minutes of Quick March, the group passed the sentries and entered the grassy field where the training day usually began.

"Form up. Dress Right. *Dress.*"

The thirty trainees formed five ranks of six each and came to Attention. Sergeant Hansen gave them a steely-eyed once over as the soldiers tried to stand as straight up as possible with their heavy back backs.

Finally, the Sergeant called out, "At Ease," followed by, "Rest, drop your loads."

No one dropped anything. The trainees' packs were set down in front of them for inspection if necessary. Their assault rifles were slung on their shoulders.

"So, Troops, did you like our nice nature hike?" asked Hansen with a bit of a smirk.

"Yes, Training Instructor!"

"That's what I like to hear. A bunch of motivated members of the Unoccupied States Armed Forces." The Sergeant glanced at her watch. "Okay. We actually finished early, which tells me you bunch of ne'er do wells are getting in shape. There is hope for you yet."

Hansen paused for a moment as she let the compliment sink in. "Alright. I want you all in the barracks with your equipment squared away by 16:30 Hours. That includes servicing your weapons. You had better clean those bores because if I find one piece of dirt or rust—you know the rest of the statement.

"You will shit, shower, and shave as necessary, put on clean BDUs, and be at chow at 17:30 Hours. I will be there eating with you, so no grab ass. Any questions?"

"No, Training Instructor." Thirty voices answered in unison.

"Atten-*tion!* Dismissed."

"*Fuck the squids!*" With the final enjoiner, the thirty humans grabbed their equipment and were assholes and elbows to the barracks.

Thirty men and women were back in their barracks bay two hours later. The Firewatch/Charge of Quarters assignment was made, and as that individual cursed their luck, the rest sat on their bunks.

The chow hall meal consisted of venison steaks with all the fixings, Bug Juice (an electrolyte-heavy sports drink), and coffee as thirst quenchers. The Free Forces leadership ensured their fighters were well-fed and fit, as they knew the War with the Tschaaa invaders would be long and hard.

Jeanie was lost in her thoughts until Big Ben—also known as B.J.—plunked down next to her on the bunk. "Squid tentacle for your thoughts, Jeanie."

Jeanie could not help but grin. Benjamin Jones was a colossal farm boy who had attached himself to Jeanie as a Battle Buddy from day one. He was Black, White, and Native American, and he had a bit of a permanent tan.

When B.J. heard that Jeanie had been close up and personal with a Tschaaa, he had pressed her for details. And when Jeanie told him her friend Indigo Dax had been grabbed because of her darker skin while Jeanie was let go, B.J. growled, *"That ain't gonna happen again. No, sir. No Squid is gonna take me or you, Jeanie. I'll rip their tentacles off."*

Jeanie knew B.J. was big and strong enough to make good on that threat. She was glad B.J. had grabbed her as a Battle Buddy. The group and barracks were co-ed, but no one thought about sex or fooling around. They did not shower together like in the movies and they had separate toilets.

However, everything else was done as a unit. There were insufficient personnel and facilities for separation. Plus, only thoughts of killing Squids were on the trainees' minds.

All had lost someone or everyone to the Tschaaa. Payback was the permanent word of the day.

"Just wondering when the training stops and the payback begins, B.J."

"Wanna hear the latest scuttlebutt?" B.J. tended to talk like a character in an old war movie.

"Sure. Why not."

"Gunny Bender is supposed to stop by tomorrow. He's healed up from that mission to kidnap a Squid."

The mission B.J. referred to was supposed to be classified. However, the word was out within a week of the survivors returning.

"Huh. It will be nice to see the Gunny again," said Jeanie.

"He's the one who recruited you," replied B.J.

"Yep. I met the missing Para Rescue Sergeant Sanchez before she left on the mission. She told me women will have to step up and fill in the slack because so many men were killed."

B.J. looked at his friend. "You planned on doing that anyway."

"Yeah. But it is still good for motivation during our field humps."

The next day was an activity Jeanie loved. The platoon paired off for combat blade and bayonet training. Jeanie seemed to have a natural affinity for cutting weapons to the point none of the trainees came close to challenging her. Thus, another Advanced Training Instructor usually came to work with her. Otherwise, Jeanie didn't get much of a workout.

As the others paired off this day, Jeanie stood At Ease and

waited for an instructor. Behind her came a familiar voice.

"Well, well. I see a former forest nymph has progressed far in her training."

Jeanie turned around and suppressed a smile as she saw Master Gunnery Sergeant Torbin Bender walk up. She came to Attention and greeted the Marine. "Master Gunnery Sergeant Bender. It is a pleasure to see you again."

"It may not be much of a pleasure, Private Parker, after I make you eat some dirt. I drew the short straw. I'm your fighting blade instructor."

Jeanie suppressed a smile. This training would allow her to show she was no longer a babe in the woods. Jeanie was allowed to keep the blade she received from her uncle, the former Marine. A military-style sheath was developed to meet uniform standards.

"Sergeant, please form a circle around the training area. I think this will be an excellent training exercise in attention to detail and individual progression."

"Yes, Gunny. All right, you heard him. Get off your buts and form a circle."

Jeannie felt all the eyes on her but was calm. She has come far since the initial meeting with Torbin Bender in the forest.

"Alright, Parker. As they used to say in France: *Engarde!*"

After a quick circling by the

two combatants, they attacked.

For five minutes, there was a back-and-forth flow of the contest between the very experienced Torbin and the competent Jeanie. Even if the weapons had not been sheathed, it wasn't very likely either person would have been cut as both were beyond capable.

Jeanie never allowed Torbin to use his size and strength, and the Gunnery Sergeant never allowed Jeanie's youth and speed to score.

Finally, just as Jeanie made a low thrust with her knife, Torbin managed a foot sweep and took Jeanie to the ground. He stood on her knife hand and pointed his K-bar at her prostrate body.

"Time!" yelled out the Sergeant.

Torbin removed his foot from Jeanie's wrist, bent over, and helped her up as he grinned. "You've been training."

"Yes, Gunny, I have."

Torbin faced the platoon. "This is what personal effort can do. This young soldier is now a dangerous person with a fighting blade. Respect her and her abilities."

Torbin offered a handshake, and Jeanie accepted as the trainees hooted and clapped in support. "You will soon have a chance at payback, Parker."

"I hope so, Gunny. I hope so."

The training platoon was allowed to turn in early after policing up the barracks. Jeannie was quickly asleep.

Sometime during the Witching Hour, Jeanie jerked awake, screaming. B.J. and Sergeant Hansen were soon at her bunk, shaking her awake. Jeanie vomited on the barracks floor as she woke up.

"I'll clean this up," said B.J.

"Parker, lean on me," said Hansen. "Head to the latrine and the showers."

Jeanie washed her face and mouth as Hansen stood by her. "Bad nightmare, Parker?"

"The worst, Training Instructor."

"If you feel like talking, let me know."

"Yes, ma'am."

Two hours later, Jeanie tip-toed towards the barracks exit, carrying her combat boots. As she quietly exited, she heard a *"Psst!"* behind her. It was B.J. "Where're you going?"

"Indigo needs me. She screamed to me."

"Jeanie, this could be seen as deserting."

"So be it. Jeanie needs me."

"I'll come with—"

"No, B.J. This is my battle.

You stay here and explain the note I left.”

“But we’re Battle Buddies.”

“And always will be. But Indigo needs me.”

B.J. hugged her. “Go with God, and come back.”

“I plan to. Fuck the Squids.”

“Fuck the Squids.”

A PERFECT SPECIMEN

ndigo Dax jerked awake from her fitful slumber on a lumpy mattress and sat up, screaming, *"Jeanie!"* She tried to jump out of the old metal bed, and fell flat on her face. The pain in her right ankle told her it was connected to the reason for her fall. A metal leg iron on her left ankle was securely fastened around the metal leg of the lower half of a former institutional bunk bed.

Indigo cursed, crawled onto the bunk, and massaged the hurting ankle. As she did, she began to think, *"Where am I?"*

The last thing she remembered was her and Jeanie in an office building, grasping tentacles, then blackness.

The door to the darkened

room opened suddenly as a tall figure strode in. A glaring overhead
light sprang to life, and Indigo covered her eyes as she tried to adjust
to the brightened interior.

"Ah, the *princess* is awake,"
sneered the male voice. It took a
few moments for Indigo's eyes to
adjust enough for her to see the
long-haired male's face was entirely
covered with a tattoo. As her eyes
adjusted more, she could make out
the detail. It was a depiction of
some multi-legged image of an oc-
topus-like creature.

"I see you noticed my hand-
some face," said the man. "Nice
tats, don't you think?"

Indigo paused in her re-
sponse as her brain processed all
the new stimuli.

"You're with the... Squids."

The large and muscular man laughed. "No shit. Remember who grabbed you? It was one of the Tschaaa warriors." The man stepped closer. "He got kudos for finding a nice piece of Dark Meat like you."

Indigo felt fury wash through her but she was smart enough not to show it.

The man reached for her manacled ankle. "Let me check. The Doctor doesn't want you injured but—"

Indigo kicked at him with her free leg. "Get off me!"

A firm grip on her throat shut off further protests and oxygen.

"That's enough, my fine Kraken friend." The new voice was from a female who just entered the room.

The identified 'Kraken' man loosened his grip, and Indigo gasped for air. Did 'Kraken' mean a collaborator? A human working with the Squids?!

"She is quite the bitch, Doctor Smith."

Indigo rubbed her throat as she looked at the new person in the room.

"Hello, young lady," said the short, forty-something, heavyset woman with wire-rimmed glasses and short dishwater blond hair. "I'm Doctor Susan Smith. I'm the one responsible for your future. I'm in control."

The Doctor paused as if to let her statements set in. "Thus, let me inform you that your stay here can be comfortable... or nasty."

"You work for the aliens," interjected Indigo.

"In a way, yes. But primarily, I continue my work concerning the human genome." Doctor Smith smiled broadly. "I so wanted to experiment on enhanced human mutations. It took an alien invasion to allow me to do so."

"Why do that?" asked Indigo.

"Why, my studies can make humans stronger, healthier, better able to survive. I could help develop super athletes."

"And make them tastier, too," the large man chuckled.

"Don, I told you not to joke like that. I am responsible for explaining the situation to our subjects. Can you understand?"

"Yes, Doctor," Don said with a crooked smile.

"Now, where was I? Okay, Indigo, I guess that is your name. You will help me with my studies. Cooperation with my activities nets you comfortable shelter, food, and other amenities."

"And I have to do what?"

"Why, you will carry a child to term while I modify its genome in the womb."

Indigo's eyes widened as the

concept sank in. "No!" she screamed. Indigo yanked at the leg iron with hysterical strength but to no avail.

"Oh, why must all of you act so hysterical? I imagine you would have an abortion if you became pregnant from a boyfriend. I performed abortions on hundreds of young women just like you. And I offered them nothing in return beyond the operation. To you, I offer a comfortable living during wartime conditions."

Indigo screamed and yanked at the restraining chain.

"Oh, damn. Don, restrain her before she damages herself. I have a strong sedative to give her. She must be calm for the artificial insemination."

"Doc, I still think you ought to let fine specimens of manhood as myself do the deed. I say, why not allow us some fun?"

Susan Smith glared at him. "I have specific standards for my work. Now, hold her down. Use a sleeper chokehold, but not too tight. That's it. Now, just enough force so I can inject her..."

Indigo did not know how long she had been unconscious. She was sore; Indigo hoped it was artificial insemination and not some Kraken's dick!

A plate of fruit and a sandwich was on the bedside table. Indigo felt hungry and quickly consumed the food. Her captives had also provided her with a bottle of water and a bedpan.

Indigo drank the water and then urinated in the bedpan. She saw a door she hoped led to a toilet. Using bedpans was not her favorite activity.

There was no metal tableware, and the food plates were paper. Indigo stretched the leg iron chain to its limit and searched the floor and table for something she could use as a shim. A former boyfriend had taught her how to escape from handcuffs by screwing with the ratchet and teeth using a shim. Despite her efforts, Indigo found nothing useful.

She laid back down and stared at the ceiling. The room had a newer paint job than most. Indigo wondered where this room was located, as there was no window, and she was not conscious when she arrived.

Indigo had just closed her eyes for a short nap when she heard a slithering she recognized. She sat up and tried to slide to the top of her bed but was prevented from doing so due to the leg iron. Indigo hefted the bedpan as the only object with some weight for use as a weapon.

Two large eyes appeared as a tentacle shoved open the room's door. The Tschaaa alien stopped at the door and stared at Indigo with unblinking eyes.

"See, My Lord, as I told you," said Susan Smith. "She is an excellent candidate for my project. She

will produce young both for my pur-
poses and yours."

"Dark Meat?" a human-like voice responded.

"Yes, My Lord. Subjects for my reproductive and growth experi-ments... and delicious meals for you and yours."

Indigo screamed.

miles away, Jeanie jerked awake and sat up. She screamed for her friend, her voice piercing the night.

"*Indigo!*"

arshall Miller is the author of the *Tschaaa Infestation* series as well as the *Agent Kim Kupar* novels (*Jade Eyes*, *The Why Files*, and *They*) inspired by Miller's own time working as a federal agent. Also the creative director and co-founder of the Kitsap Literary Artists and Writers (KLAW) creative club, Miller hosts a regular television and internet show interviewing authors and filmmakers.